BLUE MOON
SOUP SPOON

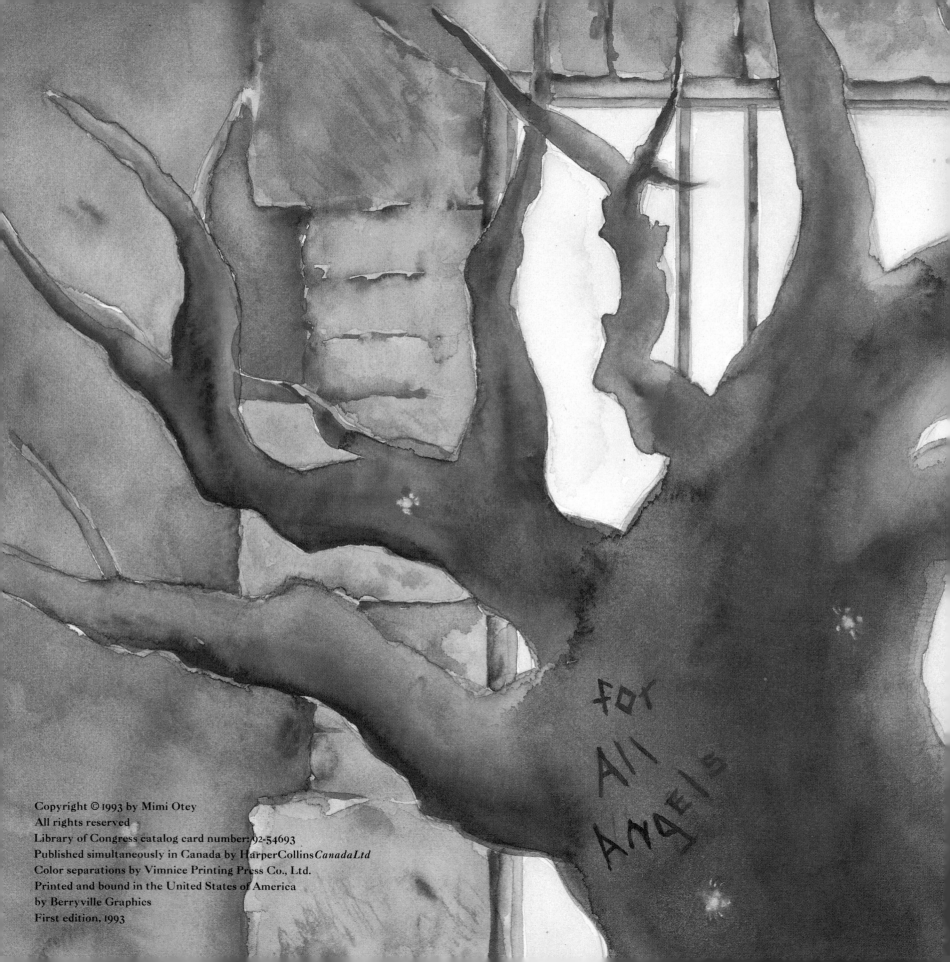

for
All
Angels

Library of Congress catalog card number: 92-54693
Published simultaneously in Canada by HarperCollins*CanadaLtd*
Color separations by Vimnice Printing Press Co., Ltd.
Printed and bound in the United States of America
by Berryville Graphics
First edition, 1993

BLUE MOON SOUP SPOON

Mimi Otey

Farrar, Straus and Giroux   New York

Blue.

Blue moon.

Blue moon spoon.

My ma.

My pa.

My moon

Sings a blue tune.

A misty, make-me-wish SHHH moon rune.

Ma's brewing stew.
Pa's home soon.

So I follow the song
out to the dune.

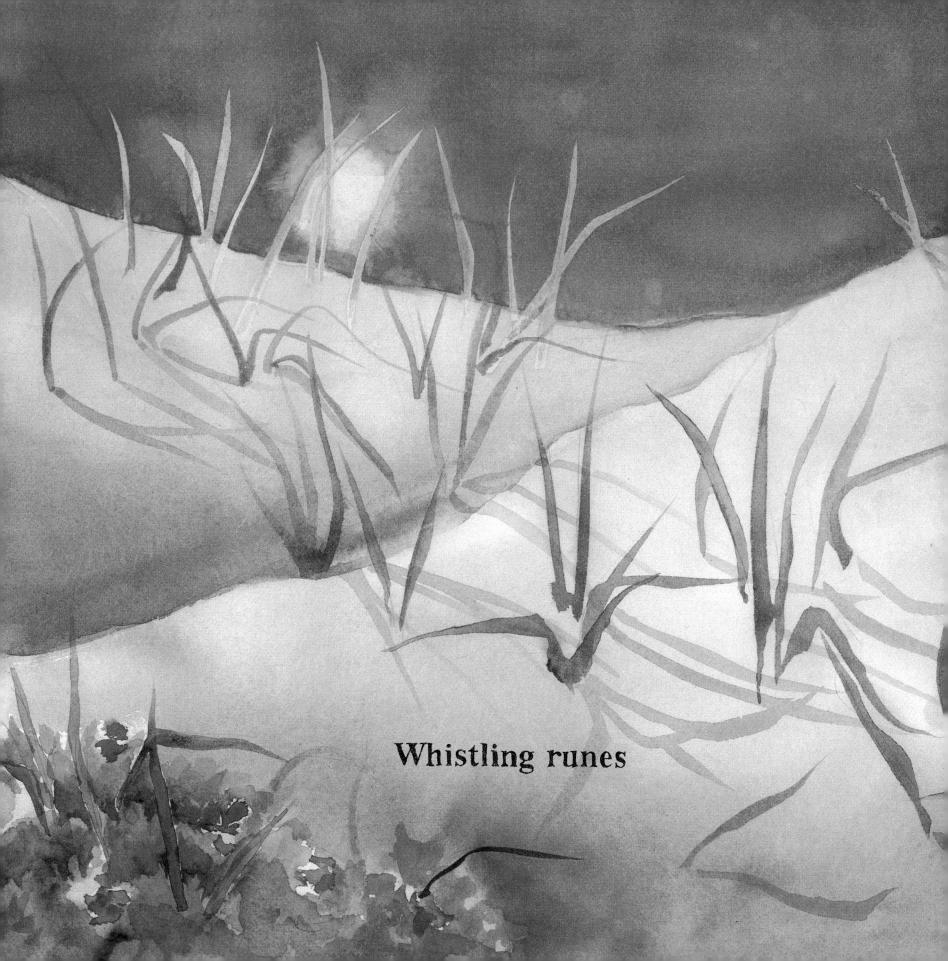

Whistling runes

traced on the hill.

A shadow looms.

Shhh.

Be still.

Pa?

Pa!

Over the dune

He comes singing a song
He learned from the moon.

My ma.
My pa.

My misty blue moon.

I eat my bean stew

With my blue moon soup spoon.